The Lime Green Secret

Written and Illustrated by

Georgia Graham

TUNDRA BOOKS

Published in Canada by Tundra Books,
75 Sherbourne Street, Toronto, Ontario M5A 2P9

Published in the United States by Tundra Books of Northern New York,
P.O. Box 1030, Plattsburgh, New York 12901

Library of Congress Control Number: 2008903002

Library and Archives Canada Cataloguing in Publication

Graham, Georgia, 1959-
The lime green secret / Georgia Graham.

ISBN 978–0–88776–841–5

I. Title.

PS8563.R33L45 2009   jC813'.54   C2008–902064–2

We acknowledge the financial support of the Government of Canada through the Book Publishing
Industry Development Program (BPIDP) and that of the Government of Ontario through the
Ontario Media Development Corporation's Ontario Book Initiative.

We further acknowledge the support of the Canada Council for the Arts and the Ontario Arts Council
for our publishing program.

ONTARIO ARTS COUNCIL
CONSEIL DES ARTS DE L'ONTARIO

Medium: chalk pastel on sanded paper

Design: Andrew Roberts

Printed in China

1 2 3 4 5 6   14 13 12 11 10 09

To Fran, the bride, and Billy, the ring bearer, forty-two years ago

–Georgia, the flower girl

The sewing machine hummed and paused, hummed and paused. Satin and ribbon flowed across the table in luxurious folds.

"You, little lady," said Mom, "are going to be the flower girl at Fran's wedding! And cousin William will be the ring bearer," she added, pointing to a tiny tuxedo.

Gloria's heart sang. She was hoping her big sister would choose her.

"Everything needs to be perfect for Fran," said Mom, with a sniff. "My baby is all grown up."

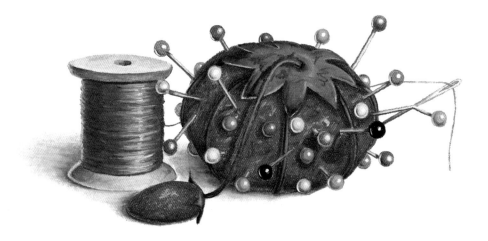

"Arms straight up!" said Mom, lifting the dress high. The gown tickled Gloria's sides as it raced to her feet. Mom tugged white gloves past Gloria's elbows. She buckled shiny white shoes over lace socks and crowned Gloria with a sparkling tiara. Then Mom quickly yanked them all off.

"Your dress stays on this hanger until the morning of the wedding," instructed Mom, placing it on a hook on the bedroom door.

Gloria couldn't take her eyes off it. At night the dress glowed like a radiant angel, hovering in the air. She rested the pristine white shoes on her pillow. Gloria couldn't wait.

Even when Gloria played, she couldn't get the wedding finery out of her head.

"I could conduct better if I were wearing high gloves," Gloria told herself, as she led an imaginary orchestra with a knitting needle. Closing her bedroom door, she slid on the gloves. Afterwards, she carefully put them back in their gold-foil box.

The next morning, Gloria couldn't bear to leave her wedding shoes behind when she went to school. As she left the house, no one noticed they were on her feet. What a wonderful echo they made as she clacked her heels on the sidewalks and in the halls! When she ran and jumped, the shoes made flashes of white.

As soon as she got home, Gloria shined them up and placed them back on her pillow. The only one who saw was her dog, Ginger.

"Sit, Ginger!" Gloria commanded, as she fitted the tiara on the dog. Ginger ran from Gloria's room, wildly shaking her head.

"No, Ginger!" The tiara flew off, hit the wall, and landed upside down. Mom appeared as Gloria was twisting it back into shape.

"Ginger did it," explained Gloria. Mom hastily scolded Gloria and then hurried off to do some wedding errands.

Gloria entertained herself by setting up a royal tea party. She put on the entire wedding outfit for Ginger.

Glancing out the window, Gloria spotted her friend. "Hey, Carolyn!" she hollered. "Wait there." With her eyes darting from side to side, she crept down the hall and past the den, where Dad was lost in a newspaper.

"Wow, the kids have got to see this!" Carolyn said, pulling Gloria's gloved arm toward the playground.

Right away, the children abandoned the teeter-totters and swings. A large group of admirers gathered around Gloria. Mark even bowed. She waved like the queen as she glided down the slide. The kids took turns pushing Gloria's swing.

Everything was fine until Gloria's cousin William appeared. "You're not supposed to wear that yet!" he said.

Gloria sped away, hurdling hedges and leaping curbs. She flew up her driveway, then crept into her house. Trembling, she collapsed against her bedroom door and dusted herself off.

"That will not happen again," Gloria vowed to her dolls and bears, who were seated around a little table. Each had a tiny teacup. In the middle was a teapot filled with lime soda pop.

"For you and you and you," she said, filling the cups, "and one for me. *Oops,* too full!" As Gloria tried to sip the soda pop, it spilled right onto the front of her beautiful gown. "Hurry," she gasped, trying to mop the spill with a doll's hair. It smeared! "Oh, no!" She dabbed it with Teddy's head, which only dried the lime green stain.

Quickly Gloria put the dress back on the hook, with the stain facing the door.

The stain loomed over Gloria like a hideous green monster. She would see it at night, when she tried to sleep. Claws splayed, hair wild, it had dozens of crazy toes going in every direction.

She worried about it all the time, even during rehearsal on the evening before the wedding. She fretted on the morning of the wedding, while her hair was being wound into tight rollers.

When a bouquet of flowers was delivered to Gloria's house, a brilliant idea popped into her head. She would hold the flowers over the lime green soda-pop stain. No one would ever know.

Three bridesmaids were waiting in the foyer of the chapel. Their dresses were identical to Gloria's, only bigger and spotless.

Heavy carved doors swung open as organ music blasted out. The chapel was filled with guests. A row of men in black tuxedos was waiting nervously at the altar. William was in front, fidgeting with the tassel on the ring pillow.

Carefully holding her bouquet in place, Gloria strode down the aisle after the bridesmaids. Aunts and grandmothers tilted their heads and smiled.

The chapel rumbled as everyone stood up. The bride and her father were entering. Fran was dazzling in her white gown. People smiled and cried at the same time.

After the ceremony, cameras were flashing everywhere. Gloria had to pose *v-e-r-y* carefully. She held her flowers in place and smiled. Then Fran and Leroy fought their way through a storm of confetti.

The reception hall was shimmering with candle-light and satin ribbons. The guests joyfully greeted each other with hugs and kisses. Gloria held the flowers over the stain and gave everyone a handshake instead. She felt sad when she didn't hug her grandma.

After the meal, friends and relatives told stories about Fran and Leroy. "When Fran was a little girl," said Uncle Gerald, "she would spill *everything,* even if the glass was glued down...." A murmur of laughter followed.

Arms entwined, Fran and Leroy fed each other wedding cake. Everyone rushed over with their cameras. Laughing, Leroy wiped icing from his nose.

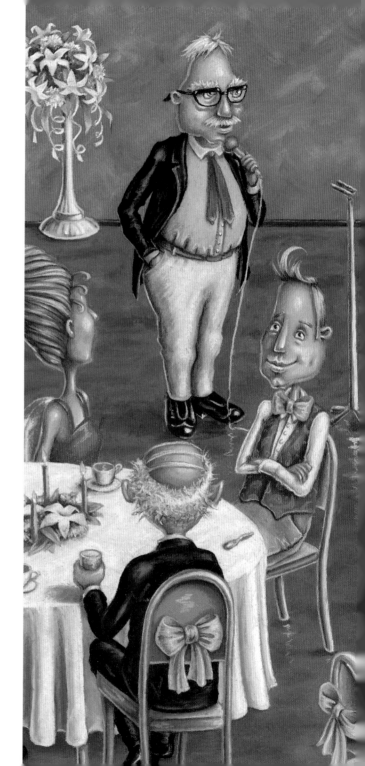

The dance floor was crowded with flailing arms and bobbing heads. Suddenly the music was interrupted by Fran's aunt at the microphone: "All single ladies to the dance floor."

"That's us," said a bridesmaid, taking Gloria by the hand.

Fran lofted her magnificent bouquet toward the group. Trailed by bouncing ribbons, it soared straight for Gloria. She kept her eyes steadily on it, dropped her own bouquet, and reached out. *Flump!* It was safe in Gloria's arms.

Fran hugged Gloria. "You and I are *so* much alike," she said.

Since the wedding, Gloria is allowed to wear the dress whenever she wants.